W9-DEZ-668

GO WEST!
Travel to the Wild Frontier

GO WEST WITH MINERS, PROSPECTORS, AND LOGGERS

Cynthia O'Brien

Crabtree Publishing Company
www.crabtreebooks.com

Crabtree Publishing Company
www.crabtreebooks.com

Author: Cynthia O'Brien
Consultant: Professor Patricia Loughlin,
   University of Central Oklahoma
Managing Editor: Tim Cooke
Designer: Lynne Lennon
Picture Manager: Sophie Mortimer
Design Manager: Keith Davis
Editorial Director: Lindsey Lowe
Project Coordinator: Kathy Middleton
Editor: Janine Deschenes
Proofreaders: Wendy Scavuzzo and Petrice Custance
Children's Publisher: Anne O'Daly
Production coordinator and Prepress techician: Tammy McGarr
Print coordinator: Katherine Bertie

Production coordinated by Brown Bear Books

Photographs:
Front Cover: **Library of Congress:** main; **Shutterstock:** br;
Thinkstock: istockphoto tr.

Interior: **Library of Congress:** 6tl, 7br, 15bl, 18br, 19, 21br, 23, 25;
Robert Hunt Library: 12bl; **Juli Scalzi:** 28br; **Shutterstock:** 6bl, Binh Thanh
Bui 17br, Everett Historical 5tr, 13, 17tr, 24tr, Gary Gilardi 18tl, Jim Parkin
7tr, Romakoma 29, Somchaij 24bl, Margaret M. Stewart 22bl, Welcomia 22tl;
Thinkstock: Betty4240 26tr, Cogent-Marketing 26br, Fuse 14, Devin Pavel
15tr, Jupiter Images 4, Ken Pilon 21tl, Urfingus 5bl; **T.J. Blackwell:** 28tl;
Topfoto: The Granger Collection 10, 11, 12r, 16, 20, 27.

All other artwork and maps **Brown Bear Books Ltd**.

Brown Bear Books has made every attempt to contact the
copyright holder. If you have any information please contact
licensing@brownbearbooks.co.uk

Library and Archives Canada Cataloguing in Publication

O'Brien, Cynthia (Cynthia J.), author
   Go West with miners, prospectors, and loggers / Cynthia
O'Brien.

(Go West! travel to the wild frontier)
Includes index.
Issued in print and electronic formats.
ISBN 978-0-7787-2328-8 (bound).--ISBN 978-0-7787-2346-2
(paperback).--ISBN 978-1-4271-1735-9 (html)

      1. Frontier and pioneer life--West (U.S.)--Juvenile literature.
2. Frontier and pioneer life--Northwest, Canadian--Juvenile
literature. 3. Miners--West (U.S.)--History--19th century--Juvenile
literature. 4. Miners--Northwest, Canadian--History--19th century--
Juvenile literature. 5. Loggers--West (U.S.)--History--19th century--
Juvenile literature. 6. Loggers--Northwest, Canadian--History--19th
century--Juvenile literature. 7. Mineral industries--West (U.S.)--
History--19th century--Juvenile literature. 8. Mineral industries--
Northwest, Canadian--History--19th century--Juvenile literature. 9.
Lumber trade--West (U.S.)--History--19th century--Juvenile literature.
10. Lumber trade--Northwest, Canadian--History--19th century--
Juvenile literature. I. Title.

F591.O37 2016   j978'.02   C2015-907972-1
                                               C2015-907973-X

Library of Congress Cataloging-in-Publication Data

Names: O'Brien, Cynthia (Cynthia J.) author.
Title: Go West with miners, prospectors, and loggers / Cynthia
   O'Brien.
Description: New York : Crabtree Publishing, 2016. | Series: Go
   West! Travel to the wild frontier | Includes index. | Description
   based on print version record and CIP data provided by
   publisher; resource not viewed.
Identifiers: LCCN 2016001530 (print) | LCCN 2015049839 (ebook)
   | ISBN 9781427117359 (electronic HTML)
   | ISBN 9780778723288 (reinforced library binding : alk. paper)
   | ISBN 9780778723462 (pbk. : alk. paper)
Subjects: LCSH: West (U.S.)--History--Juvenile literature. | Mines
   and mineral resources--West (U.S.)--History--19th century--
   Juvenile literature. | Miners--West (U.S.)--History--19th century-
   -Juvenile literature. | Logging--West (U.S.)--History--19th
   century--Juvenile literature. | Loggers--West (U.S.)--History--
   19th century--Juvenile literature.
Classification: LCC F594 (print) | LCC F594 .O245 2016 (ebook) |
   DDC 978/.02--dc23
LC record available at http://lccn.loc.gov/2016001530

Crabtree Publishing Company
www.crabtreebooks.com   1-800-387-7650

Printed in Canada/022016/IH20151223

Published in Canada
Crabtree Publishing
616 Welland Ave.
St. Catharines, Ontario
L2M 5V6

Published in the United States
Crabtree Publishing
PMB 59051
350 Fifth Avenue, 59th Floor
New York, New York 10118

Published in the United Kingdom
Crabtree Publishing
Maritime House
Basin Road North, Hove
BN41 1WR

Published in Australia
Crabtree Publishing
3 Charles Street
Coburg North
VIC, 3058

CONTENTS

What Are the Prospects?

The North American West has many natural resources. By the mid-1800s, waves of settlers had moved there to seek their fortune in lumber and precious metals.

TIMBER TURNS A PROFIT

★ **Wealth in West Coast forests**

★ **Mining towns need building material**

In the early 1800s, the **lumber** industry boomed in the forests around the Great Lakes. So much wood was cut that the forests became thin. Meanwhile, demand for lumber in the West rose after the California Gold Rush of 1849. Settlers in the West needed to build homes and stores. Oregon, Washington, and British Columbia had thick forests. Soon, logging camps and mill towns sprang up along the coast.

Right: Giant redwood and Douglas fir trees grew widely along the Pacific Coast.

DID YOU KNOW?

A prospector is someone who looks for useful or valuable minerals. A miner is someone who digs minerals out of the ground. In the 1800s, the two roles were closely related. If a prospector found gold or silver, he started digging!

Heavy Metal

★ **Not all that glitters is gold**

Gold was not the only valuable metal in the West. A silver rush began in the 1870s, with discoveries in Arizona, Colorado, and Nevada. In addition, miners found metals used in construction and manufacturing, such as iron, zinc, and copper. These metals brought wealth to many states.

Hurry, Hurry, Hurry!

★ **Latecomers miss out**

★ **Big business gets involved**

The first prospectors and miners arrived in California in the summer of 1848. Many of these "Forty-Eighters" successfully found gold in streams or near the surface of the ground. About 70,000 "Forty-Niners" arrived the following year. They found that most of the easily accessible gold was gone. Only a few of these latecomers made a fortune. Instead, most ended up working for large mining companies. From the mid-1850s, these corporations used **hydraulic** mining to extract gold.

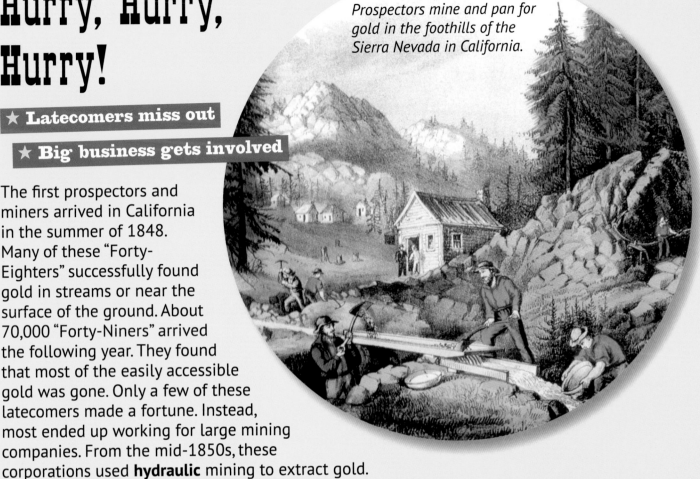

Prospectors mine and pan for gold in the foothills of the Sierra Nevada in California.

OPPORTUNITY KNOCKS

★ **California business booms**

★ **Miners have money to spend**

Some of the best ways to make money in the West had nothing to do with mining or logging. The miners and loggers who headed west needed places to stay, food to eat, and tools to work with. People quickly built hotels, restaurants, and stores to keep up with the workers' needs. These male and female **entrepreneurs** started some of the first successful businesses in the West. With little competition, they could make a lot of money.

Lure of Gold

The United States acquired California from Mexico on February 2, 1848. At that time, no one knew that gold had been discovered in California just nine days earlier.

James Marshall stands where he found gold next to his new sawmill.

WHAT'S THAT SHINY THING?

★ **Carpenter strikes it lucky**

★ **Discovery kept under wraps**

In January 1848, an accidental discovery led to an international frenzy. John Sutter, a landowner in California, had hired James Marshall to build a sawmill on the American River, near present-day Sacramento. While inspecting the site, Marshall spotted some shining flakes in the water. Tests confirmed it was gold. Sutter and Marshall agreed to keep the discovery secret, but word soon spread. The California Gold Rush had begun. Both Sutter and Marshall later lost their rights to the land. They both died penniless.

Mountain Gold Rushes

★ **Rockies gold discoveries ignite new fever**

★ **Miners brave rugged landscape**

In 1858, prospectors found gold along Cherry Creek in the Rocky Mountains, near what is now Denver, Colorado. Other mineral discoveries in Montana and Idaho followed. Thousands of miners set up camps in the mountain valleys, slopes, and surrounding plateaus. Early settlers endured harsh winters and often found little gold. When they gave up, their mining camps became ghost towns. Other camps, such as Denver, Colorado Springs, and Boulder, became cities.

GOLD IN THE HILLS

★ **Custer reports gold**

★ **Miners flock to Dakota**

Since the 1850s, rumors had circulated about gold in the Black Hills in Dakota Territory. When General George Custer led a US Army expedition into the region in 1874, he took two prospectors, who soon found gold. *The New York Times* published news of the finding in August. By the following fall, 15,000 miners had arrived in Sioux Territory.

Right: The Black Hills were sacred to the Sioux. The US government had given them ownership of the region, but did not prevent miners from moving in.

Battle for the Black Hills

★ **Great Sioux War**

★ **Custer's Last Stand**

DID YOU KNOW?

The Sioux still claim possession of the Black Hills. In the early 1920s, they began a legal case to get the land back. The case is still being argued in the law courts.

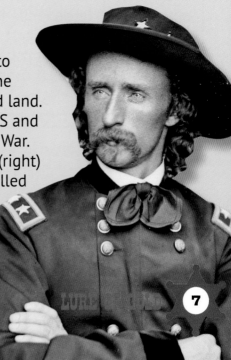

When news of Custer's discovery spread, the US government tried to gain control of the Black Hills. The Sioux refused to sell their sacred land. In 1876, tensions between the US and the Sioux led to the Great Sioux War. In the most violent clash, Custer (right) and his entire cavalry unit were killed by Lakota Sioux warriors at the Battle of the Little Bighorn in Montana. In 1877, the United States seized control of the Black Hills.

Where in the West?

Yukon

In 1896, gold was discovered in the Klondike region of Yukon in Canada. About 100,000 prospectors stampeded to the freezing wilderness. Three years later, they left to rush to a new gold strike in Nome, Alaska.

Idaho

Gold was discovered in Idaho Territory—today's states of Idaho and Montana—in 1860. Up to 20,000 prospectors soon arrived. Although it is not as well known as the California Gold Rush, the gold rush in Idaho produced more gold.

California

The accidental discovery of gold at Sutter's Mill in the foothills of the Sierra Nevada in January 1848 sparked the greatest internal movement of people in American history, as prospectors flooded to the West.

Comstock Lode

Silver was discovered under Mount Davidson in Utah Territory (now Nevada) in 1859. The find sparked a silver rush. The Comstock mines were highly profitable and were the location of many key innovations in mining technology.

Arizona

Silver was discovered in Arizona in 1877. By the early 1880s, Tombstone was a thriving town of 10,000 residents. In the early 1890s, the mines flooded. Mining became too expensive, and the boom was over.

Nome •

ALASKA

• Dawson City, Yukon

CANADA

Helena •

Deadwoo

Sutter's Mill

• Idaho City

Denve

Virginia City

• Tombston

Discoveries of gold and silver were made throughout the West, especially in the Rockies and California.

Key

—————— Major railroads

Pacific Northwest woodlands

Gold regions

Silver regions

Black Hills

Gold was discovered in the Black Hills of Dakota Territory (now South Dakota) in 1874. Although the region was sacred to the Sioux, miners moved in and settled new towns such as Hill City, Pactola, and Deadwood. The Sioux fought the Great Sioux War with the US government in an unsuccessful attempt to protect their traditional lands.

Routes to the Goldfields

Dawson City

NORTH AMERICA

San Francisco

Independence • New York

Panama

SOUTH AMERICA

Key

.... Route to Alaska

.... Route to San Francisco

———— Route to Klondike

———— Route to California

• Chicago

UNITED STATES

Rocky Mountains

Gold was discovered in July 1858 near Pikes Peak in the Rocky Mountains in Colorado. A gold rush began that lasted the next three years. One of its key effects was the growth of nearby Denver as a regional urban center.

Gold Fever in California

Getting to California from the East meant a long journey. People risked months of hardship and disease to chase dreams of a better life.

News Spreads

Above: Citizens in New York read about the Gold Rush.

★ **Mormon storeowner spreads the word**

★ **Brannan profits from mass migration**

Samuel Brannan owned a store in Sutter's Fort, near the site where gold was found. Brannan headed to San Francisco, where he flashed a bottle of gold dust, shouting, "Gold! Gold! Gold from the American River!" By mid-June 1848, three-quarters of the male population of San Francisco had left the city to head for the "diggings," or goldfields.

DID YOU KNOW?

Samuel Brannan's promotional stunt earned him a fortune. He sold miners arriving at Sutter's Fort goods from his store worth up to $5,000 a day ($100,000 today). He invested in land and became California's first millionaire.

Gone to the Diggings

★ **Stores and homes deserted**

★ **Travelers face grueling journey**

People were in a rush to get to California and strike it rich. Young men quit school and storeowners shut their stores. Those who left often posted a simple sign with the message, "Gone to the diggings." To get to California, these hopeful miners and prospectors traveled either by water or by land.

THE WATER ROUTE

★ **Taking the long way around**

★ **Passengers endure months at sea**

The sea route to California was not the first choice for most. It was expensive and it took longer than the land route. The journey from New England around South America was about 14,000 miles (22,531 km) long. It could take eight months, depending on the weather. There was a shortcut, in which sea travelers crossed the narrow neck of Panama from east to west. They risked malaria, **cholera**, and yellow fever in the jungle. Those who survived took another ship from Panama City to California.

MY WESTERN JOURNAL

You want to get in on the action in California, but you have to decide how to get there. Which route would you choose? Why is this route best for you?

THE LONG, LONG ROAD

★ **Cholera claims lives**

★ **Cross-country trail is no easy ride**

Many hopeful miners and prospectors set out on the 3,000-mile (4,800 km) route from Missouri to the West Coast. Most followed the rugged California Trail. The journey took about five months. Some lucky travelers could afford an ox-drawn covered wagon to carry their possessions. Poorer miners simply walked most of the way with only what they could carry. The long journey was hard. Many people died from starvation, or diseases such as cholera.

Right: A team of horses pulls a heavy wagon loaded with supplies for the gold-mining camps.

The Forty-Niners

California became the dream destination for people everywhere. In just a few years, the Gold Rush led to the largest mass migration in US history.

Hunt for Freedom

★ **African American success stories**

African Americans established some of the first mining **claims** in California. Some were former slaves seeking a new life. By 1852, around 2,000 African Americans lived in California. Many worked in service industries, such as cooking. Others started successful businesses. James P. Dyer opened a soap company. Mifflin Gibbs owned a shoe business. Gibbs also fought for African-American rights, such as public education.

*Left: An African-American miner uses a **sluice** to search for gold in California. Water in the sluice separates any gold from the soil.*

BURIED SHIPS

★ **San Francisco's crowded harbor**

★ **Vessels buried underground**

When gold hunters sailed to San Francisco, the ships' crews often headed to the goldfields too. By the end of 1850, some 500 ships were abandoned in Yerba Buena Cove. At least 70 ships were buried when city developers filled the cove with sand and built streets and buildings on top.

Taxing the Foreigners

★ **Mexicans stake their claims**

★ **Chinese miners arrive**

Around 6,000 Mexican miners were among the first to make claims in California, which had been part of Mexico until 1848. The Mexicans were expert miners. By the end of 1852, 20,000 Chinese miners had also arrived. American miners protested that they were being pushed out by the foreigners. In response, California forced all non-American citizens to pay a hefty tax—$20 per month (about $630 per month today).

Left: This hand-colored engraving shows life in a Chinese mining camp in California in 1857.

A MIXED CREW

★ *Sacré bleu*, here come the French!

★ California's population surges

By the mid-1850s, about 300,000 people had settled in California. Two-thirds of the newcomers were American, and most of them had traveled across the country from New England. More than half were young men in their twenties. Other fortune hunters included about 30,000 people from France and former **convicts** from Australia. The remaining immigrants came from as far away as Ireland, Germany, South Africa, Russia, and South America.

DID YOU KNOW?

The California Gold Rush was the largest in American history, but it wasn't the first. A farmer's son discovered gold in North Carolina in 1799, sparking a Gold Rush.

Seeing the Elephant

A few prospectors made their fortunes in the California Gold Rush. After the earliest days, however, the majority were disappointed.

SEEING THE ELEPHANT

★ **Fortune smiles on a few ...**

... most hopes are dashed

Hopeful miners heading to California said they were going to "see the elephant." The phrase means to see something astounding, but to pay a heavy price to do it. Few miners saw the elephant, though some were lucky. One soldier who stopped by the Mokelumne River found a huge gold **nugget** worth a fortune. However, most miners returned home penniless or found other jobs.

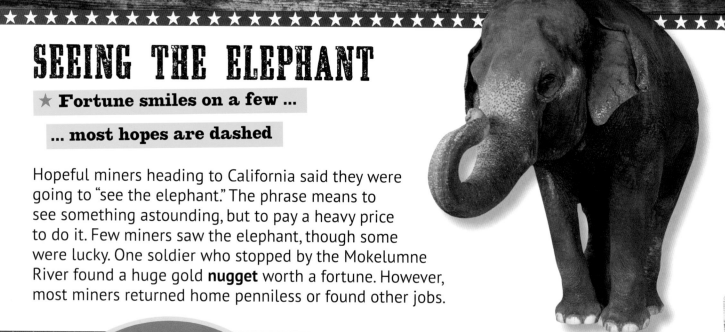

DID YOU KNOW?

Some Chinese miners hid their gold from robbers or to avoid paying heavy taxes on it. They hid the gold by melting it and making things such as pots. When they returned to China, they melted the gold into bars to sell.

Big Business

★ **Corporations see dollar signs**

★ **$81 million made in a year**

At the peak of the Gold Rush in 1852, about $81 million in gold (about $2.5 billion today) was dug out of the ground. The industry was changing, however. The **placer** gold near the surface had gone, and miners could no longer afford to work alone. Mining companies began **investing** in the industry. They paid for large crews and bought equipment to reach deep-set gold.

"WONDERFUL PANTS OF LEVIS"

★ **Tailor manufactures "waist overalls"**

★ **Miners love durable pants**

In 1850, the German tailor Levi Strauss began making wagon covers and tents for miners out of a strong cotton twill. He sold few, but had a smart idea. Using the same fabric, which came from France, Strauss started making work pants for the miners. The hard-wearing garments were so popular, he opened a factory. The fabric, which he called "serge de Nîmes," was dyed with indigo and became known as "denim." "Levis" became the first blue jeans ever made.

Right: Levi Strauss used rivets to strengthen the joins in his pants.

Supply and Demand

★ **Making money outside the mines**

★ **Fortunes to be made in retail**

Most miners arrived in California with few supplies. Merchants took advantage of the increased demand for goods. The price of food, clothing, and other basics went up dramatically. Even a blanket cost as much as $100—that's $3,000 in today's money.

A miner directs a jet of water from a pump to wash away a hillside in search of gold.

STREAMS OF GOLD

★ **Early methods require patience**

★ **Waterpower speeds things up**

Early prospectors panned for gold. This involved scooping up mud and water, and swirling the pan to separate any gold. Water was also passed through sluice boxes, which caught any gold particles in a screen. Early hydraulic mining shot river water through funnels and hoses to blast away earth banks to expose gold.

Life in the Camps

As miners arrived in the gold fields of California, they set up camps. Early settlements of tents were replaced by hastily built wooden towns.

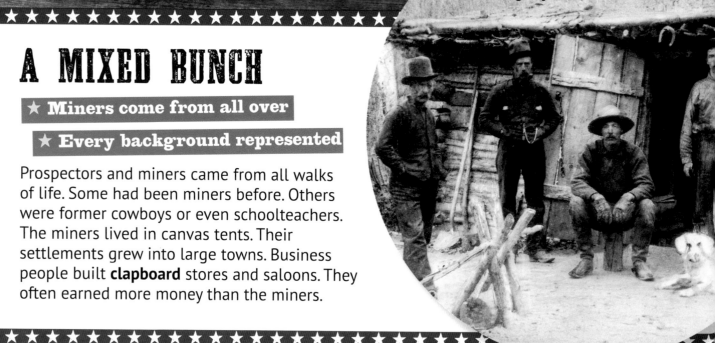

A group of gold hunters pose outside the log cabin they share in the goldfields.

A MIXED BUNCH

★ **Miners come from all over**

★ **Every background represented**

Prospectors and miners came from all walks of life. Some had been miners before. Others were former cowboys or even schoolteachers. The miners lived in canvas tents. Their settlements grew into large towns. Business people built **clapboard** stores and saloons. They often earned more money than the miners.

A Family Affair

★ **More men than women**

★ **Women stake their claims**

Far more men than women made their way to the goldfields. In the town of Rich Bar, California, for example, there were only five women among thousands of men. Sometimes wives accompanied their husbands to work a claim. In fact, a family could have twice as much land if both husband and wife each staked a claim.

DID YOU KNOW?

Lotta Crabtree began dancing, singing, and playing banjo to entertain miners in 1855, when she was only eight. She later moved to San Francisco, then to New York. Celebrated as "the Nation's Darling," Lotta made a fortune as an actress before she retired.

Keep Off My Land!

- ★ **Miners lose claims**
- ★ **Safety in numbers**

When prospectors or miners arrived at the goldfields, they made a "claim" to a piece of land. There was little law and order: miners simply chose where to start digging for gold. However, "claim jumping" was a common threat. If a prospector or miner left his claim for any reason, someone else seized it and started working. Miners began to work together to protect each other's sites. If one miner had to go into town, for example, another would watch his site.

Miners work together to pan for gold in a stream in California.

CHINESE MINERS

- ★ **Crossing the Pacific**
- ★ **Welcome to Gold Mountain**

One of the largest groups of immigrants in the West were the Chinese. In the decade after the California Gold Rush, about 66,000 Chinese immigrants arrived. Half settled there, and many moved east into Montana and Nevada to look for work. Some were miners. Many also worked on railroad construction. Chinese immigrants often lived in the same area in city neighborhoods called Chinatowns. Many still exist today. The Chinese faced racial **discrimination**, but that did not stop them. The West had so many opportunities for jobs, it was known as "Gold Mountain" in China.

What's on the Menu?

- ★ **Food prices hit record highs**
- ★ **Eat mush or go hungry**

Most miners and prospectors ate out in saloons and tent cookhouses, or cooked basic meals in their camp. They also hunted and fished. Buying food soon became a luxury. Stores charged up to $1 for a slice of bread, so miners ate an unappetizing, but cheap, blend of flour, cornmeal, and sour milk. Fresh fruit and vegetables were scarce, and thousands of miners died of **scurvy**.

Mineral Wealth

Gold was not the only valuable product to come out of the ground in the West. Silver was also found, while other metals and minerals mined there had more practical uses.

The Rocky Mountains contain deposits of many metals and minerals.

THE ROCKY MOUNTAINS

★ **New gold rushes**

★ **Valuable metals everywhere**

The Rocky Mountains stretch over 3,000 miles (4,828 km) through the West, from Canada in the North to Mexico in the South. After the 1848 California Gold Rush, some disappointed miners headed to the mountains in the hope of striking gold. Beginning in 1859, gold was discovered in Colorado, Idaho, Montana, and British Columbia. The Rockies produced far more gold than California. There were also significant deposits of lead, and of silver and copper, which were often found close to one another.

MY WESTERN JOURNAL

If you were a miner, would you prefer to pan for gold in California, or try mining in Death Valley? On what would you base your decision?

What's Found Where?

★ **Wide range of minerals**

★ **Desert states grow rich**

Metals and minerals were found throughout the West. There were large deposits of gold, silver, copper, lead, and zinc in what are now Utah and Nevada. These regions also had useful **minerals** such as clay and phosphates, which are used to make fertilizer. Southern California produced high-quality gemstones.

White Gold

★ **Valuable mineral discovered**

★ **Death Valley becomes mining hotspot**

Death Valley is the lowest, driest, and hottest spot in North America. Mountains surround a valley of sand dunes, rocky outcrops, and vast salt flats. Native Americans lived there for thousands of years, but few white settlers stayed there long. Then, borax was discovered there. Also called "white gold," borax is a mineral used in detergents and manufacturing processes. In 1883, Harmony Borax Works opened a borax mine in Death Valley. Soon, miners were braving the valley's harsh conditions to dig not only for gold, silver, and other metals, but also to search for borax.

"OLD PANCAKE" LOSES OUT

★ **New silver rush**

★ **Comstock gets nothing**

In the 1850s, Henry Comstock, who was known as "Old Pancake," had laid claim to some land left by other miners in Nevada. Gold miners complained about the "blue mud" on the land. Comstock sold his claim, not realizing that the blue mud was actually silver! The deposit was the largest source of silver in American history. Miners arrived quickly. By 1882, the Comstock Lode had produced more than $300 million in gold and silver.

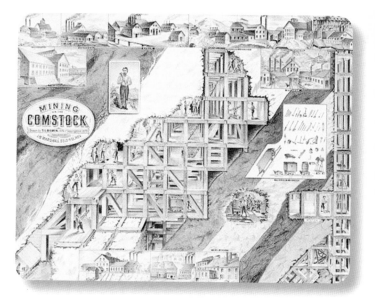

Below: This diagram shows a cutaway of the mines in the Comstock Lode.

Life for the Miners

Miners worked hard in some of the harshest environments anywhere in North America.

Miners in the Mud

⭐ **Hunger and dysentery in the camp**

⭐ **Long hours for little reward**

Even young men found mining hard work. They worked most of the day, digging and standing in cold water. On a good day, a miner might find enough gold to pay for food. **Nutritious** food was expensive, so miners often did without. Keeping clean was not a priority, and many miners got diseases such as **dysentery**. Other diseases, such as smallpox, spread quickly around mining camps.

Above:
Miners take a break underground. Conditions were hot and cramped.

LIFE IN DEATH VALLEY

⭐ **Death Valley's golden age**

⭐ **Miners build towns in the desert**

The Timbisha Shoshone Nation has lived in Death Valley for centuries. However, the **badlands** and salt flats (left) were not welcoming to settlers. The miners who arrived after 1883 built towns near their mines. They relied on water from springs at places such as Furnace Creek and Stovepipe Wells. By the early 1900s, mines closed and people deserted Death Valley's **boomtowns**.

BEAST OF BURDEN

★ Mules take the weight
★ Mexicans are expert packers

At the beginning of the Gold Rush, there were no roads or railroads in the West. Supplies had to be carried long distances to remote mining centers. Mexican *arrieros*, or mule drivers, carried supplies on pack mules fitted with saddles made from straw-stuffed leather bags. A mule could carry a load of up to 350 pounds (159 kg). Oxen were slower than mules, but cheaper. A team of oxen could pull a whole wagon full of supplies.

MY WESTERN JOURNAL

Where in the West would you choose to work and settle? Would you choose the mountains, or a mill town on the coast? What are the pros and cons of settling in a developing city such as Denver?

DID YOU KNOW?

As Denver grew, its businesses supplied the surrounding mines and their workers. It became a major stop on the stagecoach route and later on the railroad.

Next Stop: Denver!

★ Mining camp becomes trade center

The first prospectors arrived in Denver in 1858 to look for gold. Soon, tents and wagons lined the South Platte River and Cherry Creek. When gold was discovered farther into the Rocky Mountains, most miners deserted Denver. Later, many gave up on mining and returned from the mountains to start businesses in Denver's milder climate.

This photograph shows Denver in 1898, just 40 years after it was settled.

Boomtowns

Where minerals were discovered, whole towns sprang up. When the minerals ran out, however, the towns were abandoned as quickly as they had been built.

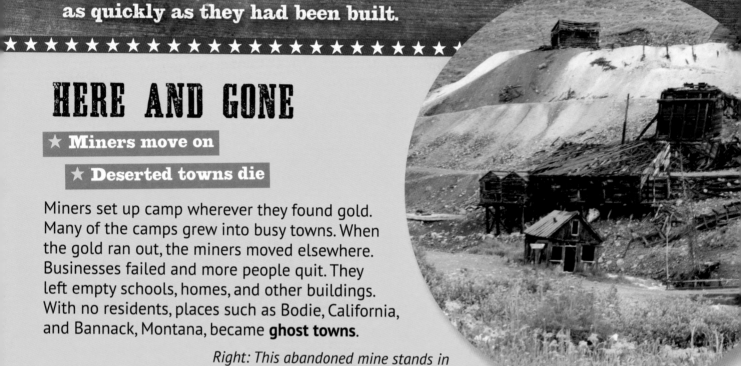

HERE AND GONE

★ **Miners move on**

★ **Deserted towns die**

Miners set up camp wherever they found gold. Many of the camps grew into busy towns. When the gold ran out, the miners moved elsewhere. Businesses failed and more people quit. They left empty schools, homes, and other buildings. With no residents, places such as Bodie, California, and Bannack, Montana, became **ghost towns**.

Right: This abandoned mine stands in the ghost town of Animas Forks, Colorado.

DID YOU KNOW?

Luzena Wilson came to California with her husband in 1849. She made money selling food to miners, and opened a hotel. When it burned down, she opened another—then another. She became prosperous and later wrote her memoirs.

Where Are the Women?

★ **Few women venture west**

★ **Worth their weight in gold**

During the Gold Rush, women represented 8 percent of the population. Men who were bad cooks paid well for a meal cooked by a woman. Many of the first women in the West made money this way. In Placerville, Lucy Stoddard Wakefield's pies were so popular she made about $240 per week ($7,590 today).

STORES ON MAIN STREET

* **GENERAL STORE:** Usually the first store in any settlement.

* **BUTCHER:** Selling tame or wild meat. Bear steak anyone?

* **DRUG AND CIGAR STORE:** Selling medicines and cigars. That's it.

* **SALOON:** Every town had at least one—but you're too young to go inside.

* **GROCERS:** For tinned and sacked food. Fresh vegetables only in season.

* **OUTFITTERS:** Get your boots, shirts, coats, pants, and hats.

* **EXPRESS OFFICE:** Communications center for receiving and sending parcels and mail by stagecoach.

Entertaining the Miners

The Eagle Theater in Sacramento opened in 1849. Eager miners paid $5 per ticket (about $140 in today's money). The theater was subject to flooding, however, and closed after just 10 weeks. Traveling entertainers, such as actress Lola Montez, put on shows at mining camps. Most of the time, professional entertainers were unavailable. Miners put on plays or musical performances themselves. Everyone enjoyed them— even if they were terrible.

Towns such as Placerville and Forbestown, California, were abandoned when the gold ran out.

THE STORY OF PLACERVILLE

★ **A typical boomtown**

★ **Ends in failure**

Placerville was the first gold camp set up in California in 1848. It was first named Dry Diggin's and later Hangtown, after three criminals were hanged there. In 1854, its name changed to Placerville. The town had a bank, a general store, and hotels. It stood on key road and railroad routes. Once the gold ran out, however, the town was abandoned in 1873.

Wealth of the Forests

The growth of settlement in the West created a huge demand for construction materials. The most popular was lumber from the forests of the Northwest.

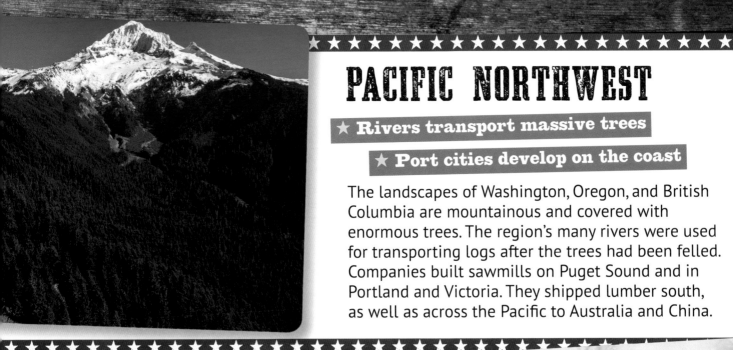

PACIFIC NORTHWEST

★ **Rivers transport massive trees**

★ **Port cities develop on the coast**

The landscapes of Washington, Oregon, and British Columbia are mountainous and covered with enormous trees. The region's many rivers were used for transporting logs after the trees had been felled. Companies built sawmills on Puget Sound and in Portland and Victoria. They shipped lumber south, as well as across the Pacific to Australia and China.

Move It!

★ **Have you seen a saw?**

★ **Stream power and steam power**

Getting lumber to the sawmill was not easy. At first, loggers felled trees beside rivers. They tied the trunks together and floated them downstream in huge rafts. If they were working farther away from the river, loggers used oxen to pull timber to it. Beginning in the 1880s, special steam trains carried the lumber.

Right: Steam rises from engines as they pull felled trees through the forest.

★ **Thousands of trees needed**

★ **Western species fill the bill**

In 1863, construction began on the Western Pacific and Central Pacific railroads. Construction on the Canadian Pacific Railroad followed in the 1880s. Railroad builders needed lumber for **ties** and **trestles**. Logging companies set up camps in the Western forests of ponderosa pine, California redwood, and Douglas fir. Their wood was more resistant to decay than wood of other trees.

Left: This railroad trestle bridge was built in 1868 in Salt Lake Valley, part of what is now Utah.

DID YOU KNOW?

Before they felled a tree, lumberjacks hacked out a large notch near its base. They then sawed through the trunk. The notch made sure the tree fell in the right direction.

Woodworkers

★ **Mill owners rake in money**

★ **Europeans bring skills to camp**

Loggers worked hard, but were paid quite well. Some were former miners who had been unsuccessful at the goldfields. Many were Native Americans. After the Gold Rush, Irish, Scandinavian, Scottish, and French-Canadian loggers joined the camps. As settlers arrived in the West and construction boomed, timber was in increasing demand. Mill owners could make a lot of money. They set up sawmills in mining areas, and supplied lumber to the miners to use as **props** inside the mines.

Life with the Loggers

Loggers lived in camps of log huts deep in the woods. Their lives were hard and dangerous. They had few home comforts and little entertainment.

LIFE WITH THE LOGGERS

★ **Shhh! No talking!**

★ **Living on the move**

Loggers lived in camps in the forest. After cutting the timber in one area, they moved on to another camp. Up to 200 men shared a camp. They slept in dirty, crowded, wooden bunkhouses. Loggers ate a lot of food to build up enough energy to work 10 or 12 hours a day. To speed up meal times, they developed a tradition of eating in silence.

Right: Loggers rest in their hut in a logging camp in the 1860s.

DID YOU KNOW?

By the 1880s, loggers' competitions were regular events. The contests grew into modern events such as the Lumberjack World Championship held in Hayward, Wisconsin.

First One to the Top!

★ **Loggers show off special skills**

★ **Competitions become a camp tradition**

Loggers held competitions as a way to pass the time and test their skills. One of the earliest events was birling. Two loggers jumped on a log in the river and rolled it with their feet. Whoever kept their balance the longest was the winner. Other contests involved tree climbing, ax throwing, and wood chopping.

★ Not much of a library

Logging camps were isolated from the world. There was little to read. Letters from home took a long time to arrive. The men treasured them, reading them again and again. Often, the only book to read might be a farmer's almanac. This popular yearly publication contained astronomical predictions and weather forecasts for the year.

WATCH OUT FOR FALLING TREES

★ Danger on the job ...

... and in camp!

Falling trees and accidents with tools injured or killed many loggers. They were not the only dangers faced by loggers, however. When they were in camp, loggers often had to go for weeks or months without changing their clothes or washing properly. Cramped bunkhouses meant that diseases, such as pneumonia, spread fast. Lice and bedbugs were also common.

Right: Loggers pose on the stump of a huge fir tree, with the long saw they used to fell it.

Shaping the West

The rush to gather valuable natural resources in the 1800s had a lasting impact on the development of the West. Its influence is still visible today.

The Morenci Mine in Arizona is one of the largest copper mines in the world.

MODERN MINING

- ★ Mining on a massive scale
- ★ Pits are open for business

The West is still a huge source of minerals. Western states supply most of America's copper and silver. Borax is produced in California, and uranium used in atomic energy is mined in Wyoming. Gold comes from **open-pit mines** in Nevada. Western provinces in Canada still mine gold, silver, and uranium, as well as diamonds in the Northwest Territories.

Boomtown in the West

- ★ City is still growing
- ★ Heart of the mountains

In 2009, a survey found that Denver was the most popular American city to live in. The old mining town had more than 660,000 residents in 2014. Its location between the Midwest and the West Coast made it an important media, business, and transportation center. It is still home to many energy and mining companies.

The Tourist West

DID YOU KNOW?

The first tourist resort in Death Valley was a tent village in the early 1920s. Later that decade, a borax mining company turned its crew accommodation into a resort. These two early resorts are now the valley's main tourist centers: Stovepipe Wells and Furnace Creek.

Today, the most valuable resources of the West include its natural beauty and history, which attract hundreds of thousands of tourists. Among the most popular sites are those linked to the region's past. In California, visitors can explore the lives of borax miners in Death Valley or walk among the redwoods in Sequoia and Kings Canyon national parks. The Gold Region in the foothills of the Sierra Nevada is also popular, as is Virginia City in the heart of the Comstock Lode of Nevada. Tourists also visit the Klondike Gold Rush National Historical Park, which borders Alaska and Yukon.

LOGGING TODAY

★ **World's largest producer**

★ **Wood still wanted**

The United States is the largest producer of lumber in the world, followed by Canada. Much of the North American lumber comes from the forests of the Pacific Northwest in Oregon, Washington, and British Columbia. Although machines such as the electric chain saw have made logging easier, handling huge trees remains dangerous. Loggers still have to venture deep into the forest, and rafts of logs are still floated down rivers to ports such as Portland, Oregon, and Vancouver, British Columbia. More than 500,000 people work in the industry.

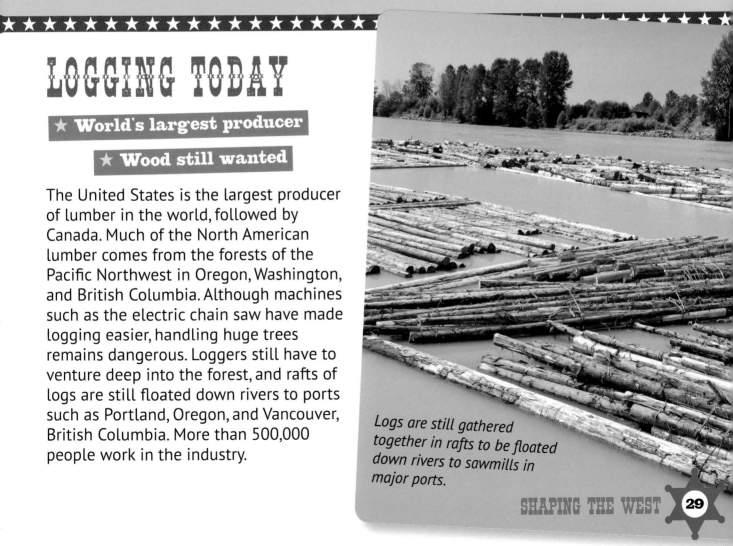

Logs are still gathered together in rafts to be floated down rivers to sawmills in major ports.

GLOSSARY

badlands Regions of eroded land with little vegetation

boomtowns Communities that grow rapidly because of sudden prosperity

cholera A serious infectious disease, usually caused by drinking dirty water

claims Pieces of mining land that individuals chose and worked on

clapboard Overlapping planks of wood used as building walls

convicts People who have been imprisoned for committing crimes

discrimination The unjust treatment of a group of people, often on the grounds of their race or sex

dysentery A serious infection of the intestines causing severe diarrhea

entrepreneurs People who take risks by setting up businesses

ghost towns Abandoned settlements

hydraulic Powered by a fluid that is under pressure

investing Putting money into a venture in hope of a later profit

lumber Wood that has been cut into pieces that are ready for use

minerals Solid natural substances that have never been alive

nugget A usually small, naturally occuring lump of gold or other precious metal

nutritious Describing food that is needed to help animals or people stay healthy and grow

open-pit mine A mine in which minerals are dug from a huge pit

placer Deposits of sand or gravel in lakes or streams that contain particles of valuable minerals

props Beams used to hold up the ceiling of a tunnel

scurvy A serious disease caused by a lack of vitamin C

sluice A channel with a controlled flow of water through it

ties Long wooden blocks that support the rails of a railroad

trestles Open frameworks of timbers used to support bridges

January 24: James Marshall discovers gold at Sutter's Mill in the Sierra Nevada foothills in California.

Around 70,000 "Forty-Niners" arrive in California from elsewhere in the United States and around the world.

July: Gold is found near Pikes Peak in what is now Colorado, starting a gold rush in the Rocky Mountains.

Spring: Silver is discovered in the Comstock Lode near Virginia City, in what was then part of Utah Territory.

1848 **1849** **1852** **1858** **1859** **1860**

February 2: California passes from Mexico to the United States under the Treaty of Guadalupe Hidalgo.

About 20,000 Chinese arrive in California. They are made to pay a Foreign Miners Tax.

November 22: Denver is settled as a mining town near Pikes Peak.

October: Gold is discovered on Orofino Creek in Idaho, sparking a gold rush.

ON THE WEB

http://www.history.com/shows/ax-men/articles/history-of-logging
A page from History.com with a video about the history of logging.

http://www.wisconsinhistory.org/turningpoints/tp-027/?action=more_essay
Gives information on the "turning points" in logging history with fascinating primary sources to explore.

http://www.onlinenevada.org/articles/comstock-lode
Detailed article from the Online Nevada Encyclopedia about the Comstock Lode.

http://www.history.com/topics/gold-rush-of-1849
History.com page on the California Gold Rush, with links and videos.

BOOKS

Friedman, Mel. *The California Gold Rush* (True Books). Children's Press, 2010.

Holub, Joan. *What Was the Gold Rush?* Turtleback, 2013.

Landau, Elaine. *The Gold Rush in California: Would You Catch Gold Fever?* (What Would You Do?) Enslow Elementary, 2015.

Olson, Tod. *How to Get Rich in the California Gold Rush*. National Geographic Children's Books, 2008.

November 7: Denver is incorporated as Denver City; it becomes capital of the new Colorado Territory.

August: On a US Army expedition to the Black Hills in Dakota Territory, General George A. Custer discovers gold, beginning a gold rush.

August: Silver is discovered by Ed Schieffelin in Arizona. The resulting silver rush creates the boomtown of Tombstone.

1861   **1872**   **1874**   **1876**   **1877**   **1896**

November: Gold is found near Sitka in Alaska.

Partially to protect their land in the Black Hills from mining, the Lakota Sioux and their allies go to war with the US government; they are defeated the next year.

August 16: Gold is discovered in Yukon in the Klondike region of northwest Canada. The last great Gold Rush of the American West begins the following year.

INDEX